A WOODLAND MYSTERY

The Woodlanders Begin

A WOODLAND MYSTERY
By Irene Schultz

D1177934

**Wright Group
McGraw-Hill**

To dear friends Kelvyn Lilley and Marcella
Slezak

The Woodlanders Begin
Copyright ©2000 Wright Group/McGraw-Hill
Text by Irene Schultz
Cover illustrations by Meg Aubrey
Cameo illustrations by Taylor Bruce
Interior illustrations by Tom Sperling and Adam Weiskind

Woodland Mysteries® is a registered trademark of
Wright Group/McGraw-Hill.

Wright Group/McGraw-Hill
19201 120th Avenue NE, Suite 100
Bothell, WA 98011
www.WrightGroup.com

Printed in the United States of America

10 9 8 7 6 5 4 3

ISBN: 0-322-01955-9
ISBN: 0-322-02368-8 (6-pack)

What family solves mysteries ... has adventures all over the world ... and loves oatmeal cookies?

It's the Woodlanders!

Sammy Westburg (10 years old)
His sister Kathy Westburg (13)
His brother Bill Westburg (14)
His best friend Dave Briggs (16)
His best grown-up friend Mrs. Tandy
And Mop, their little dog!

The children all lost their parents, but with Mrs. Tandy have made their own family.

Why are they called the Woodlanders? Because they live in a big house in the Bluff Lake woods. On Woodland Street!

Together they find fun, mystery, and adventure. What are they up to now?

Read on!

Meet the Woodlanders!

Sammy Westburg
Sammy is a ten-year-old wonder! He's big for his fifth-grade class, and big-mouthed, too. He has wild hair and makes awful spider faces. Even so, you can't help liking him.

Bill Westburg
Bill, fourteen, is friendly and strong, and only one inch taller than his brother Sammy. He loves Sammy, but pokes him to make him be quiet! He's in junior high.

Kathy Westburg
Kathy, thirteen, is small, shy, and smart. She wants to be a doctor someday! She loves to be with Dave, and her brothers kid her about it. She's in junior high, too.

Dave Briggs

Dave, sixteen, is tall and blond. He can't walk, so he uses a wheelchair and drives a special car. He likes coaching high-school sports, solving mysteries, and reading. And Kathy!

Mrs. Tandy

Sometimes the kids call her Mrs. T. She's Becky Tandy, their tall, thin, caring friend. She's always ready for a new adventure, and for making cookies!

Mop

Mop is the family's little tan dog. Sometimes they have to leave him behind with friends. But he'd much rather be running after Sammy.

Table of Contents

Table of Contents

Chapter 1:
Children Alone

One hot morning, three children sat on the front steps of a big house in the woods.

They looked sad.

The door behind them was open a crack. They didn't see the woman behind it, spying on them.

The children had lived in the house for only one night. They were brothers and sister, even though they were all adopted.

Bill was the oldest of the Westburgs. He was almost fourteen, and short for his age. He was strong and kind.

"So how do you like Uncle Ted's house, Kathy?" he asked.

She answered, "The house is fine, but I miss Mom and Dad." Tears came to her eyes as she spoke.

Kathy was thirteen. She had blue eyes and braces on her teeth.

Sammy, their ten-year-old brother, said, "I don't see why they had to fly with Uncle Ted to Africa in the first place, and get killed. It's not fair.

"And that Mrs. Tandy! She looks mean, like a tiger. I don't trust her.

"Why did the judge send us to Bluff Lake to live with her, anyway?"

Bill said, "She kept house for Uncle Ted. And with Mom and Dad and Uncle Ted dead, there was no one else for us to live with. But I think she'll be OK.

"What I worry about is when school starts.

"I bet I'm the only one with brown skin in this town. And I'm always the shortest in my grade."

"Don't worry," Kathy said. "You'd make good friends here even if you were bright green instead of brown.

"I wish I were friendly like you.

"I get shy sometimes, so kids think I'm stuck up. And these braces don't help!"

Suddenly, Sammy looked up. "You think short is bad?" he said.

"How would you like to be the biggest kid in fifth grade, like me? I'm a giant! And I can never get my hair to look right."

It was true: Sammy's hair was always a mess.

Bill poked Sammy lightly and said, "Cheer up. That's not so bad. You're OK, Sammy."

Sammy poked Bill back ... HARD! He looked MAD! He stood up.

Bill stood up, too. The boys looked about the same size. Sammy was only one inch shorter than his older brother.

Kathy said, "Cool down, both of you."

Sammy sat down again, slowly, and snorted.

Bill snorted back.

Then Sammy stuck out his tongue at Bill.

Bill stuck out his tongue at Sammy.

The two of them began snorting ... and sticking out their tongues ... faster and faster. Finally, all three kids broke out in giggles.

Bill stopped laughing and said, "Come on, let's explore."

Mrs. Tandy shut the door in back of them without a sound. She was afraid they might catch her spying.

But the children didn't see her.

They walked around the house to the back, where the woods were the thickest.

"Hey, look! A rabbit!" said Bill. He ran after it.

"I hope Mop won't get it," Sammy said.

Kathy said, "Don't worry. The rabbit is safe. Mop is in the house."

Bill called, "Hey, here's a path in the woods!"

Sammy said, "Let's walk down it and see where it goes."

Kathy said, "Oh good! It's so dark and quiet. We can pretend we are wolves hunting for deer."

The three children began to pick their way into the dark woods. They tried not to make a sound.

At first, they could hear only birds and the wind.

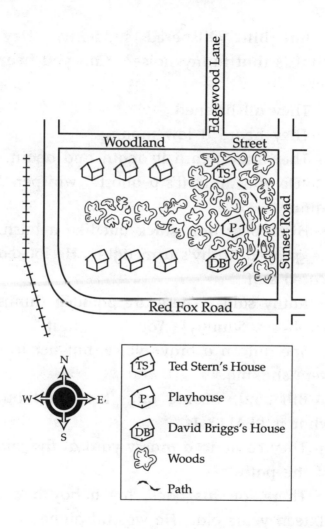

N
W — E
S

TS Ted Stern's House

P Playhouse

DB David Briggs's House

Woods

Path

But Bill whispered suddenly, "Hey, what is that funny noise? Can you hear it?"

They all listened.

They heard a low moan.

Then they heard it again and again.

"Do you think it's a ghost?" whispered Sammy.

His brown hair stuck out like a bush. He gripped Kathy's arm tight. He looked scared stiff.

Kathy said, "There are no such things as ghosts, Sammy! You know that!"

She put on a brave voice, but her legs were shaking.

Bill said, "Come on. Let's find out what it REALLY is."

They came to a grassy yard at the end of the path.

There, on his back, lay a boy about sixteen years old. He was all alone on a cot.

He was moaning softly, with one arm over his eyes.

"That's the sound we heard," Kathy whispered.

"He hasn't seen us. Let's go away. I'd hate to have someone see me when I was crying."

They began to back away.

Just then, they heard twigs snapping loudly in the woods behind them.

Before they could grab him, a small shaggy dog shot past.

He ran right into the yard where the boy lay.

It was their dog, Mop!

He raced all around the cot.

He barked.

He hopped on his hind legs just like a circus dog.

He darted up to the boy and licked his face.

The boy stopped moaning. He laughed and wiped his face.

Then the dog ran zig-zag across the yard.

"Catch him!" shouted Bill. He and Sammy ran out of the woods after Mop.

"How did he get out?"

Kathy stepped out of the woods, too. She wanted to tell the boy that she was sorry they had sneaked up on him.

He turned his head to look at her.

She saw he had blond hair and big, strong arms. He was the nicest looking boy she had ever seen.

He was dressed in shorts. His legs looked funny. They were very skinny, with twisted toes.

Shyly, Kathy tried to talk. "I—I ... We ... my brothers and I ... we ... ."

Just then, Sammy gave a loud shout.

Mop got scared. He fell flat on his belly. Bill grabbed him up.

"This is our dog, Mop," he said to the boy. "He ran off."

Sammy added, "We just moved into Ted Stern's house last night. He was our uncle.

"We didn't want to run into your yard. But we had to catch Mop, or he'd get lost. Are you mad at us?"

Kathy looked down at her feet and blushed.

The boy still lay on his back, but slowly his face broke into a big smile.

He said, "I'm not mad. I'm so glad you have come. I've been waiting for you for six weeks."

The children stared at him with their mouths open in surprise.

They had never seen him before in their lives! Why was he waiting for them?

Chapter 2:
The Old Clubhouse

The boy said, "I'm Dave Briggs. I live here with a man who helps me."

He pointed to a metal chair tipped over on the grass. It had big wheels on the side.

"Will you stand that up next to me, please?"

Bill lifted the wheelchair.

"What's wrong?" Sammy blurted out. "Did you break your legs?"

"No, my neck. I can't walk anymore."

"Is that why you were crying?" asked Sammy.

Kathy and Bill both poked Sammy, to shut him up.

"Leave me alone! Stop poking me!" Sammy cried out.

He ducked away from them.

Dave said, "Don't be upset with him. I WAS crying because I was so lonesome.

"Let's sit down. We have a lot to talk about."

He leaned over the side of the cot to grab his wheelchair. He pulled himself into it, dragging his legs after him.

14

Bill, Kathy, and Sammy sat down on the grass near him.

Dave said, "You must be Bill Westburg, and you must be Kathy, and you're Sammy."

"But how do you know about us?" Bill asked.

Dave answered, "MY family was killed in the same car crash that hurt me.

"When your Uncle Ted heard I was in the hospital, he came to see me ... every day for six months.

"When I got home, he still came over. He was my best friend, like a second father. He even took me to his jewelry shop every day."

Sammy asked, "Did he tell you about us? About me?

"We are all adopted. Our mom and dad adopted us because they wanted children ... but mostly me," he bragged.

15

"I'm the best one."

Dave laughed.

"Yes, he told me about all of you. And after the plane crash killed Ted and your folks, I hoped you might move here."

"Why?" asked Bill.

"I knew that Ted's house would belong to you.

"And Mrs. Tandy, who was Uncle Ted's housekeeper, is here, and there are good schools.

"But I began to worry. Today, I gave up on you and I felt so lonely."

Bill said, "Well, you're the best news we've had in weeks. It's nice to have a friend in a new place."

"Yes," Kathy agreed softly.

Sammy walked over to Dave. He stuck out a finger and poked Dave's leg.

"Can you feel me doing that?" he asked.

16

Kathy blushed, she was so upset. "Sammy!" she said.

Dave said, "No, I can't feel that."

"How about this?" Sammy poked Dave's other leg.

"Nope."

Bill shouted, "Stop it, Sammy! You're being a pest."

"Who's a pest?" Sammy said.

He pouted his lips and squinted at Bill. He looked ready to fight.

Bill said, "Don't give me the evil eye. And don't go around like a woodpecker, tapping on people."

"If I were a woodpecker, I'd go after your HEAD," said Sammy.

"Hey, you two, wait a minute," Dave said. "Here are the four of us alone, with no parents. We should be friends and not fighting."

Bill said, "You're right. I know that.

17

It's just that I take one look at Sammy and I get so boiling mad.

"He's always sticking out his tongue at me.

"Or taking apart something of mine that takes two hours to put back together.

"Or falling on my head.

"Or squirting me from the bathtub with a plastic bottle.

"Or throwing a gym shoe at me.

"I love him, but he's hard to take."

Sammy laughed. "I forgot about the gym shoe," he said. "That was a good one!"

"I know what you mean," Dave said softly. "I had a little brother, too, until the smash-up."

"Well, now I'M here," Sammy said. "When Bill gets sick of me, I'll come over and see you.

"I can be your part-time brother. Bill will be glad to get me off his hands some of the time.

"Besides," he went on, "Bill started it that day with the squirt bottle. He splashed me, by mistake. I had to get even.

"And I don't really pester him THAT much ... ."

Then Sammy tickled Kathy's ear with a piece of grass until she pushed him away. He began walking around Dave's yard.

"Hey, what's this?" he called. He had come to a play house half hidden by bushes.

Its white paint was peeling and its front step was split.

"That used to be our playhouse," Dave said sadly.

"It would make a fine clubhouse," said Bill.

"Hey, why don't we fix it up, and make up a secret club?" Sammy shouted.

Dave said, "I WOULD like to use it again."

Bill said, "I'll build a ramp so you can wheel inside."

Kathy said, "And we can paint it."

Sammy said, "I can wash the windows. I used to help my mom do that," he added sadly.

But Kathy got so excited she forgot to be sad or shy.

She said, "I'll make new curtains ... and help paint.

Bill said, "It will be great. When can we start?"

Kathy said, "What's wrong with today?"

Dave said, "That's a great idea! Bill, will you go to the back door and tell my helper that you're my friend? Tell him to give you my keys. His name is Mr. Cook."

Bill said, "Here, Sammy. Hold Mop."

He ran to the door.

He knocked on it again and again. No one answered.

At last, Dave called, "Go upstairs and look on the dresser in the first bedroom."

In a little while, Bill came out with the keys.

Dave said, "I wonder where Mr. Cook went. Oh, well, let's go open up our new clubhouse."

But as they crossed the lawn, he was thinking. "I've known Mr. Cook for a year now, and yet I always have the feeling that I can't quite trust him.

"Something's not right here. But it can wait until later," he thought.

But he was wrong. It wouldn't wait.

Chapter 3:
Making Plans

Bill had to try the key a few times to make the rusty lock work.

Even in the bright morning sun, the playhouse was dark inside.

The windows were gray with dust.

Spider webs filled every corner and hung from the ceiling.

Mice had chewed on the pillows and table legs.

Dust lay on everything.

"YUCK!" Sammy said. "It looks like Bill's room at home ... except this is neater."

Kathy said, "When we get it cleaned up, it will be a lot lighter."

Bill said, "Let's make a list of what we need to fix it up."

Sammy said, "But how will we bring it all back from the store?"

Bill said, "Will your helper drive us, Dave? Or maybe we can walk back and carry everything if it isn't too far."

"Don't worry," Dave said. "Your Uncle Ted taught me how to drive. I have a car with hand controls."

Dave took a piece of paper and a pencil from his pocket. "I'll write out a list."

Bill said, "I'll need boards to make the ramp."

Kathy said, "Write down white paint. A gallon."

"And we will need about ten yards of cloth for the pillows and curtains," Kathy said. "And pillow stuffing and paintbrushes."

Bill said, "We will need nails and a hammer."

Dave said, "I've got those here and ... my mother's sewing machine ... soap and rags ... and pails for water."

"Why are you so quiet, Sammy?" asked Bill.

Sammy said, "I was thinking what we should buy. Maybe a cat to get rid of the mice, and a frog to eat the spiders."

The others laughed.

Dave said, "OH, BY THE WAY! I have something important to tell you.

"Somewhere in your uncle's house, a lot of jewels are hidden.

"A few hours before he left for Africa, a huge shipment of jewels came by mail.

"The bank was closed. He told me he'd have to hide them in his house until he got back."

"WOW!" Sammy said. "What were they like?"

"They were mostly big diamonds. One was as long as my little finger ... almost. There were yellow and pink diamonds, too.

"And he had some emeralds. One was as big as a walnut. It was carved to look like a man's head."

Sammy said, "Cool! What else was there?"

"There were star sapphires, blue and smooth. And red rubies, and big pearls.

"He said he had a hiding place safe from any robber.

"Now no one knows about the jewels but us. They belong to you, if we can find them."

All of a sudden, Bill stood up and pointed.

"Did you see something move in the woods? I think someone's hiding near that dead tree."

Bill ran into the woods but no one was there. Then he leaned down and picked something up.

"Someone WAS here," he called.

Sammy asked, "How do you know?"

Bill said, "I'll show you in a minute."

He had a creepy feeling, as if a bug were crawling up the back of his head.

Was someone watching him as he walked away out of the woods?

Chapter 4:
Fixing Up the Clubhouse

Bill came back to the yard with a man's wallet in his hand. Inside was some money, but no ID card with a name on it.

They counted the money.

Dave said, "That could be someone's pay for a week!"

"WOW!" Bill said. "Whoever it was has lost a lot of money!"

Sammy asked, "Can we keep it? Is it ours now? Because no one had the right to snoop on us?"

Bill answered, "We don't know for sure it was a snooper. Anyway, the money isn't ours."

Dave said, "I suppose someone might have been lost in the woods. Then he might have gotten scared and run off."

Sammy said, "Finders keepers, losers weepers. I still say the money is ours. Bill, you're just trying to stop me from being rich."

He made a fist at Bill and made his poison-spider face.

"Oh, stop already," said Bill. "If you

scare me too much I'll faint right on top of you."

Sammy pushed Mop into Kathy's arms. He grabbed Bill like a mad gorilla.

Kathy said, "Careful, Sammy! Don't squash him."

Dave said, "I'll tell you what. Later, I'll call Police Chief Hemster and report the lost wallet to him. He will tell us what to do."

"You have a HAMSTER for a police chief in Bluff Lake?" exclaimed Sammy. "What are the firefighters, goldfish?"

Dave said, "It's HEMSTER, not hamster." He laughed.

"Now put Mop into my car. We will buy a long chain for him. Then while we work, he can run around."

They drove to the stores and bought what they needed. They chose yellow and white cloth.

Bill said, "It's pretty, and it's on sale. What luck!"

When they got back, Bill went up to the house again. This time Dave's helper was there.

"Hello," Bill said.

"Hello, kid," said the helper, with a mean look. "What do you want?"

Right away Bill knew he did not like Mr. Cook. He hated being called "kid."

Mr. Cook was quite tall. He had wavy light brown hair and blue eyes.

Bill looked him right in the eye. "I'm Bill Westburg. I'm a friend of Dave's. He asked me to have you bring the sewing machine out to the porch."

"Oh, right away, young man," Mr. Cook said. "If you're a friend of Dave's, you're all right with me."

Bill told him the other things they needed.

Then they began.

First, Sammy pounded a post into the yard for Mop's chain.

Then Bill read the booklet to get the sewing machine going. But when he couldn't figure it out, Kathy took over.

35

Bill and Sammy swept out the playhouse, even the walls and ceiling.

Then they washed the windows, with Sammy inside and Bill out. Sammy made awful faces as they worked.

"I'm practicing to scare the snooper," he said.

Dave said, "He'd drop over dead if he saw that last face you made."

Bill laughed. "You mean the one where he stretched his eyes and mouth with his hands ... stuck out his tongue until his tonsils showed ... and crossed his eyes?"

Kathy said, "I'd make a worse face, I'm getting so hungry."

"Me, too," said Bill and Dave at the same time.

Just as they spoke, Bill and Dave saw a slim figure walking toward them from Dave's driveway.

It was Mrs. Tandy.

She had a huge basket hanging from her arm.

"I thought I'd find you all at Dave's house. Children and dogs like to run off into the woods.

"Anyway, here's your lunch. There's some for Dave, too."

She put down the basket and began to walk away.

"Thank you," they called after her.

"Be back for dinner at six," she said sharply. Then she was gone.

Kathy spread out the large red and white cloth from the basket.

Dave lifted his footrests and lowered himself onto the grass.

They un-wrapped their sandwiches. There were ...

four chicken

four egg salad

... and four peanut butter and jelly.

There were ...

apples

cupcakes

milk

... and paper cups and napkins.

For about five minutes, there was no talk, only munching.

"Boy, this was NICE of her!" Sammy said when he came up for air.

"She looked like a meany when we first met her, but now I think she's even a little pretty."

Kathy said, "I was really hungry. But at last I know how to work that sewing machine.

"At first I dropped the spools.

"I put the thread in backward.

"I broke a needle.

"I spilled oil on my socks.

"I cut one curtain crooked.

"Then, by mistake I sewed a scrap of cloth to a curtain, and had to rip it out."

Dave handed her a chocolate kiss from the bottom of the picnic basket.

"You're the sewing hero of the morning," he said. "And besides, you've been talking without blushing."

Kathy blushed.

Sammy said, "Hey, what about me? I did all that cleaning even though there were lots of spiders in there!"

Dave said, "OK! Here's a chocolate kiss for you, funny-face of the week.

"And Bill, here's one for best wallet-finder. Mine is for best boss. Now back to work, all of you!"

Bill finished the ramp. Then they all painted the outside of the clubhouse.

They decided to paint the chairs and table, too.

Bill took out all the old paint cans from Dave's basement. They ended up with one black chair, one red chair, one blue chair, and a green one.

They painted the table yellow.

They were so proud of their outside paint job, they painted the inside walls white, too.

By 5:30, they were really tired. And they were all done.

Dave had Mr. Cook come out to help

them clean up.

The children sat in a row on the grass, looking at the fresh, white clubhouse.

It looked just like a real house, only smaller.

Dave said, "It's perfect! I had no idea we could get it all done in a day."

Bill said, "What should we call it? I'll make a sign for it."

Sammy said, "We should have a name for our club, and that's what we should call our clubhouse."

Kathy said, "Our houses are both in a woodland. We could be the Woodlanders."

Sammy said, "You know, that's a pretty good name!"

"I like it," Bill said.

"So do I," said Dave.

Before they went home, Bill painted THE WOODLANDERS on a board and nailed it above the clubhouse door.

"Come over after dinner," Dave called as they walked into the woods.

"We will figure out how to find the jewels."

Chapter 5:
The Great Jewel Hunt

"Dave asked us to come back," Bill said to Mrs. Tandy after dinner.

"Don't get lost," she answered. "Wait, take these with you."

She handed them each a big flashlight. They were the square kind you could set on a table.

"Give one to Dave, too," she said. "Always carry them when you go to his house and back. Those woods are dark. And take Mop with you."

"Gee, thanks," said Sammy. "I love it." He kissed his flashlight.

He took Mop's leash down from a hook near the back door. Mop began to yip and dance on his hind legs.

Outside, Sammy said, "I wonder why Mrs. Tandy wants us to have such bright lights. There aren't any bad animals in these woods, are there?"

Bill said, "No. Why does she worry so much? Doesn't she ever smile?"

Kathy said, "I don't think she's mean at all. She just has something on her mind."

44

He looked at them and smiled. "And tomorrow is Saturday," he said.

Sammy asked, "How will we get your chair into our place?"

Dave said, "It's only one step up onto the back porch.

"And Ted always took me down the ramp when we wanted to go to the basement."

Bill said, "Sammy and I can manage all that. We are very strong."

"I'm the strongest," Sammy bragged.

Kathy said, "Where do you think we should start our hunt?"

Bill said, "Let's list every place we can think of."

"First, there's the basement," said Dave. "It's really big. There's an office at one end. The basement runs under all of the house except Ted's bedroom. That bedroom was added on last year."

47

Bill said, "I'll list all the rooms. There's Uncle Ted's bedroom ...
the living room
the kitchen
the dining room
the hall
Sammy's and my room
Kathy's room
Mrs. Tandy's room
Uncle Ted's bath room
Mrs. Tandy's bath room
our bath room
... and Uncle Ted's walk-in closet."

Sammy said, "Don't forget to list the attic ...
the garage
the loft above the garage
the front porch
... and the back porch."

"Wow," said Bill. "This sounds like it's going to take a long time."

Dave said, "We can all make check lists so we don't forget to look everywhere."

They wrote this:

Look under, in, on top of, behind, and on sides of ...

drawers and shelves

rugs and furniture

pots, pans, vases

bowls, boxes, cases

clothing and shoes

door and window frames

radios and things like that

... and pictures.

Jewels may be mixed with small things.

Tap on all walls and ceilings.

Bill said, "I think we should work in pairs. That way we can remind each other where to look."

"Can I hunt with Dave?" Sammy begged.

49

Kathy said, "That sounds like a good way to begin."

Dave said, "We will change partners each day."

Bill said, "I think we are all set to start. We will come to get you at ten after eight in the morning, Dave."

Sammy said, "And bring your new flashlight."

Kathy said, "Let's go right to bed. We need to be wide awake in the morning for the Great Jewel Hunt!"

Then they waved good-bye and went off into the dark woods.

Chapter 6:
The Muddy Footprint

The next morning, after Mrs. Tandy was gone, Kathy and Sammy waited with Mop in their yard.

Soon Dave came wheeling down

Sunset Road. Bill was jogging along beside him.

"Wow," Sammy said. "You're pretty fast, Dave.

"Or maybe Bill's just pretty slow."

Bill ignored him. He said, "Mr. Cook sure wanted to come with us. He asked three times before we left."

Dave said, "I know. Your Uncle Ted and I hired Mr. Cook a year ago.

"Mr. Cook tried to do everything for me, but Ted put a stop to that.

"Ted said that if Mr. Cook really wanted to help me, he'd show me how to do things on my own."

"Here's the path to the back of our house," Bill said.

Kathy and Sammy helped get Dave down the basement ramp. Dave held back on the big wheels, to keep the chair from going too fast.

Sammy's hair was un-combed. He said that Saturdays were for rest, and he was resting his hair.

When they got to the basement, he kept jumping up and down and saying, "Come on! Come on! Let's start!"

Bill said, "Hey, I thought you wanted to rest?"

Sammy said, "Just my hair, not my brain."

Kathy and Bill began to hunt in the main basement room. At one end, there were bookshelves along one whole wall.

"You'll have to take out every book, I'm afraid," said Dave.

"Ted could have used hollow books for hiding places."

"Come on, Sammy," Dave said. "We can start in the office."

For about two hours, there were sounds of things being moved and put back in place, papers rustling, and walls being tapped.

By then, Dave and Sammy had moved back into the main basement room.

They searched the bumper pool table and some boxes.

They looked in the stuffed fishes hanging on the wall.

They looked all over the two couches.

Finally, Sammy sat down on one of the couches.

"I quit," he said. "We'll never find them."

Dave said, "Let's all rest for a few minutes and talk. Maybe Kathy and Bill can think of something we missed in the office."

While they were talking, Kathy suddenly whispered, "Keep on talking, all of you. I think I hear footsteps upstairs. I'm going to take a look."

"Be careful," Dave whispered.

Bill said, "I'll go with you."

Together, Kathy and Bill crept up the steps.

Just when they got to the top step, they heard some one move across the dining room.

They tip-toed across the kitchen and

jumped out into the dining room. A man stood there.

Bill said, "MR. COOK! What are you doing here?"

It seemed to Kathy the man looked like a trapped animal.

Then he smiled at Bill and said, "My, you scared me, Bill! I was so worried about Dave. I dropped in to make sure he was OK."

Bill asked, "But Mr. Cook, how did you get in here?"

Mr. Cook said, "Oh, Mr. Stern gave me a key to his house long ago. He wanted me to check on things when Mrs. Tandy was out.

"Well, I'll be going now. Bye!"

Bill went downstairs and told the others what happened.

Dave said, "It's funny Ted never told me about giving a key to Mr. Cook. Well, let's get back to work."

They looked all over the rest of the basement.

They were part way through the workshop when Sammy said, "Do you know what time it is? It's two-thirty! I'm starving!"

Kathy said, "Mrs. Tandy left lots of food in the refrigerator. Let's look."

They found ham ...,

butter

tomatoes

bread

grape jelly

... and chocolate milk.

As they were eating, Kathy said, "It's too bad Ted didn't tell you where he hid the jewels."

Bill said, "It's not just too bad, it's funny he didn't."

Sammy said, "Well, if you ask me,

57

something else is funny, too." He licked the jelly from a spoon and then pointed it at a window.

On the ledge under the window were big chunks of mud. And on the floor below was a big, muddy, man's footprint.

"Mr. Cook lied about how he got in," Sammy said.

Kathy asked, "Why?"

Dave looked worried. "I don't know why he would do that."

Sammy waved his fist. "I'll go to

Dave's house, and wrestle Mr. Cook down, and sit on him.

"Then Bill can ask him why he lied."

Bill laughed. Sammy was trying to sound so tough.

Bill said, "He could always say he came to check on Dave."

Kathy said, "And he made up the story about having the key because he was surprised. He didn't know what else to say."

Dave said, "I think we will have to lock all the windows from now on, to keep Mr. Cook out."

It was 3:30 by now. Kathy and Bill cleaned up the food.

Dave and Sammy went around and locked the windows.

"Now no one can snoop on us," said Sammy, as they went back down to the basement.

They all went into the workshop. They looked through the woodpile.

They looked into every box and jar above it.

They looked all around the furnace.

They searched every inch of the storeroom.

They looked behind every can of food.

Then Sammy whispered, "Here we go again. I hear someone upstairs."

Dave said, "No way! That can't be! We locked everything up."

Sammy said, "But listen!"

Sure enough, they heard creaking footsteps.

Dave said, "That makes me MAD! How did he get in?"

Sammy asked in a shaky voice, "What if he comes downstairs this time?"

Kathy whispered, "What if he tries to hurt us?"

Dave whispered suddenly, "Into the closet, guys. All of us."

They dashed without a sound into the big, dark, walk-in closet. Old clothes hung inside. There was a door at each end.

Dave said, "Quick, shut the doors. Everyone take a blanket off that shelf. Hand me one."

He flashed his light up.

He went on. "If he opens the door, everyone throw your blanket right over his head. Here, two of us should stay at this door, and two of us at the other one."

The children shivered back against the old clothes.

They could hear the footsteps come slowly through the kitchen above.

Then, one by one, the footsteps came down the wooden stairs.

They came tap, tap, tapping across the basement floor, closer and closer to the closet door.

THEN THE DOOR FLEW OPEN!

"NOW!" Dave shouted.

They all threw their blankets. It was a blanket storm.

Bill jumped forward and grabbed the wiggling heap of blankets. "I've got him!" Bill yelled.

"Help! Murder! Police!" screamed a voice from inside the blankets.

It was a woman's voice!

It wasn't Mr. Cook at all!

They had caught Mrs. Tandy inside the blankets!

Chapter 7:
A Bad Surprise for
Mrs. Tandy

Now everyone was yelling at once.

Mrs. Tandy screamed, "Help! Murder! Let me go!"

Bill yelled, "OH, NO! Get these blankets off of her! Hurry!" He tried to un-wrap her.

Kathy yelled, "We're so sorry, Mrs. Tandy! We didn't know it was you!"

Dave yelled, "What are you doing here on a Saturday?"

Sammy shouted, "Now we are in for it! We thought you were someone trying to hurt us!"

Everybody was tripping over blankets in the dark closet.

Sammy had the good sense to think of pulling the light cord.

But he was so excited, he pulled too hard. The string broke in his hand.

He groaned, "Now I broke the light cord!" He switched on his flashlight.

He saw Bill grin. Bill was thinking how funny they all looked.

But Sammy got mad. "Stop laughing at me!" he yelled.

He made a flying tackle but missed Bill. He pulled down an armful of clothes on top of his head.

Bill laughed. "Cut that out, Sammy. Let's clean up this mess!"

At last, Mrs. Tandy spoke again. "For goodness sakes! Who did you think I was? A burglar?"

She sounded upset, but not angry.

She went on, "Lucky someone didn't break a leg in this mess. Looks like I did the smart thing ... coming back when I did.

"Something's going on. Everybody knows about it except me."

Then she said, "And whatever you're looking for, good luck. I think it's going to be very hard to find.

"Because someone very tricky has been over every inch of this house already, looking.

"Now let's go upstairs and get some cocoa into all of us."

She looked at Sammy. "Just give me the light cord. I can fix it."

Sammy said, "Mrs. Tandy, you are SO nice, not to be madder at us. I used to think you were mean. But that was the day before yesterday, when I didn't know you.

"But now I know I was wrong. So today I'll help you make the cocoa."

Mrs. Tandy said, "The idea of cocoa sure has changed your mind about me fast!" She grinned.

Bill said, "Kathy and Dave and I will pick up this mess."

Mrs. Tandy and Sammy went upstairs.

Soon, Bill and Kathy had put the last blanket back on the shelf.

Bill said, "Who do you think Mrs. Tandy was talking about, Dave? You're

the only one Uncle Ted told about the jewels, right?"

Dave said, "I have my own ideas, but let's wait to hear what she says."

As they sat around the table, Bill said, "Mrs. Tandy, who's been looking here besides us?"

Mrs. Tandy said, "I have to tell you a story, so you'll understand.

"It begins when I was a child. My mother had a baby boy.

"As he got older, he did bad things all the time. Not little things, but things that hurt other people.

"When he was a young man, he even went to jail. He had used a gun and robbed somebody.

"When he got out of jail, he left town. We never heard from him after that.

"Then my folks died. I tried to find my brother.

"I was hoping he had changed for the better. But I had no luck finding him.

"Then one day, about six months ago, I was out for a walk. I'd never met the man hired to help Dave.

"He never came here to meet me.

"That day when I saw him with Dave, he reminded me a bit of my brother."

Dave said, "WHAT? Why didn't you say anything?"

Mrs. Tandy said, "I couldn't be sure.

It had been more than twenty years, and people change."

Mrs. Tandy went on. "Anyway, before I could say anything, Dave said, 'This is Al Cook, my helper.'

"Well, my brother's name wasn't Al Cook. It was Fred Wilson.

"So I decided I must have been wrong, that it was not my brother. After all, I hadn't seen my brother since I was young.

"Mr. Cook only nodded and said he was glad to meet me, so then I thought I could be mistaken."

Sammy asked, "So tell us, was he your brother, or not?"

Mrs. Tandy said, "I tried to see Mr. Cook again, but he was always busy ... so I didn't know at first.

"I feared that if he was my brother, he was up to something bad.

"I was scared for Dave. Yet, I knew

your Uncle Ted was watching out for him. It was easier to believe that Mr. Cook was NOT my brother.

"But a few nights after Ted died, I heard a tap on the door.

"I asked who it was, and a voice said, 'It's me, Becky. Let me in, Sis.'

"It WAS my brother, using a fake name. He told me that now that Ted was dead, he was going to take charge of both houses.

"He said he overheard Ted telling Dave about a hiding place. He said that he was going to find out what was hidden there before anyone else did.

"And he had a letter for you, Dave, from Ted! My brother said he wasn't going to give it to you."

"A letter!" the children all cried out at once.

"Yes, mailed to Dave the night your uncle left."

"Did he show it to you?" Dave wanted to know.

Mrs. Tandy said, "No. But he said it was in some sort of code.

"He told me he had come to Bluff Lake in the first place to get money from me when he needed it.

"By chance, he saw Ted's ad for a helper for Dave. He felt the job was perfect for him.

71

"If Dave came to depend on him, my brother would have it easy for life.

"He knew I'd try to stop him if I found out. He said now I'd better go along with his plans or I'd be sorry."

Dave said, "What in the world did you tell him?"

Mrs. Tandy said, "Tell him! I chased him out the door!

"I told him to take good care of you, Dave, or I'd call the police."

Sammy said, "But weren't you afraid he might try to hurt you?"

Mrs. Tandy said, "A little. But I was more afraid for Dave.

"Just before he left, he said, 'If you go to the police, Dave will suffer.'

"Then he stamped off."

She sighed. "I knew he was as good as his word, and I just didn't know what to do."

Chapter 8:
A Good Surprise for
Mrs. Tandy

Dave asked, "Why didn't you come to ME
... when you knew Al Cook was really
your brother?"

Mrs. Tandy said, "I was going to. But then I decided that I would watch over Dave ... until you all were here.

"Meanwhile, my brother has been searching this house."

Bill asked, "How does he get in?"

Mrs. Tandy said, "Well, the day before yesterday, I found the lock broken on the basement door.

"And someone had gone through Ted's things. I think it must have been my brother."

Dave said, "Well, Mrs. Tandy, WE know what he's looking for. And I bet he knows now.

"Yesterday, I told Kathy and Bill and Sammy that Ted had hidden some jewels here. Somebody was listening in the woods. It must have been Mr. Cook."

Sammy said, "He will go crazy for sure now. He's looking for millions in jewels, and he doesn't have one dollar to his name ... because he lost his wallet.

"Serves him right for stealing Dave's letter."

Dave said, "We should talk to Chief Hemster, but what proof do we have?"

Kathy said, "I think we are looking for the wrong thing in the wrong house."

Dave asked, "What do you mean?"

Kathy said, "We should find Uncle Ted's letter first. We might never find the jewels without it."

Bill said, "What if Mr. Cook keeps the letter on him? We've got to search through Dave's house, AND Mr. Cook's clothes for the letter."

"Aw, come on," said Sammy. "How are we going to get him out of Dave's house AND out of his clothes?"

Mrs. Tandy said, "I know how to get him out of Dave's house."

"How?" everyone asked.

"Get him here!"

"That's perfect," Dave said. "Tell him I told you about the jewels hidden here.

"Tell him you decided to help him find them, to get half for yourself."

"You can keep him here for hours that way," Kathy said, "while we hunt for the letter at Dave's place."

Bill said, "And I know how we can see if he carries Dave's letter on him.

"We will be in the yard tomorrow when he's leaving to come here. We will dump paint on him by ACCIDENT.

"He will have to take his things off in the garage to change."

Sammy said, "Then we sneak a look in his pockets when he goes inside to change."

"All right," Dave said. "Tomorrow morning let's do it."

Mrs. Tandy said, "There is something else we have to talk about. I don't want you going back to your house tonight, Dave. You might not be safe there."

"Well," said Bill, "you can call Mr. Cook and tell him Dave's spending the night with us.

"And tell him that you've changed your mind about helping him.

"I bet he will agree to anything you say ... when he hears about the jewels."

That's just what Mrs. Tandy did.

Later, when Dave was out of the room, Mrs. Tandy talked quickly.

"Children," she said, "I know Dave should never go back to living in that house with my brother. I've been thinking ... ."

"I bet I know what you've been thinking, Mrs. Tandy," Bill broke in.

"I bet I do, too," Kathy said.

"Me, too," Sammy added. "Why can't Dave live with us, here in this house?"

"That's it!" said Mrs. Tandy and Bill and Kathy. "Why can't he? Let's go find him and ask him if he wants to."

But before they could ask him, Dave came back into the room.

He said, "I want to ask you something.

"I was wondering if, until I can find someone else to live with me, I could stay here. Would it be too much trouble?"

They all began to laugh and talk at once, asking him to stay with them forever.

Suddenly, Sammy stopped. He said, "Hey, Mrs. Tandy, what's wrong?"

Big tears were rolling down Mrs. Tandy's cheeks, and she was looking for her hanky.

She finally found it and blew her nose. "I just wish Ted were here," she said. "I know he would have been so glad to have Dave living here with this family."

Later, as they all made dinner, Mrs. Tandy didn't notice the children sneaking around and whispering. But she found a surprise on her plate when they all sat down to eat.

Sammy said, "That's because you don't boss us around, and because you are brave and smart. And you sure can cook, too," he said, stuffing a muffin into his mouth.

The surprise was a bright yellow badge. Written across it were these words:

MRS. TANDY

New Member of the Woodlanders Club

Chapter 9:
The Hunt for the Letter

The next morning, everyone got up early.

By the time they were dressed, Sammy and Bill had breakfast cooking.

They made blueberry muffins ...
fried eggs
milk
oranges
... and melon pieces.

Sammy said, "We wanted to make breakfast for you, Mrs. Tandy."

He had a squashed blueberry stuck to his chin.

He also had on his worst torn T-shirt, and his cut-off jeans. He was dressed for painting ... or paint SPILLING, to be exact.

After breakfast, the children went to Dave's backyard.

The plan was simple. Bill would climb up on the clubhouse roof and pretend to be painting the trim. Dave would sit below and watch.

When Mr. Cook came out, he would stop to talk to Dave.

Sammy would trip and fall against Mr. Cook, and push him toward the clubhouse. Bill would drop the paint can at the same moment, right onto Mr. Cook.

Dave whispered, "Here he comes. All set?"

"Right," said Bill.

A moment later, Mr. Cook had white paint down one whole side of his shirt and pants.

He shouted at Bill, "You little brat! You did that on PURPOSE! I'm going to make you sorry you ..."

Mr. Cook got no further, because Sammy started shouting. "Don't you call my brother names, you rotten sneak, you ..."

Bill jumped down from the clubhouse roof and clamped his hand over Sammy's mouth.

"Don't listen to my brother," he said. "No wonder you're mad. I'm really sorry about the mess with that paint, Mr. Cook. Here's a rag. Maybe we can wipe some of it off."

He began wiping Mr. Cook's shoulder. "Sammy," Bill said, looking hard at his brother, "go help Kathy, right now."

Sammy backed slowly away from Bill. He said, "But Bill, he ..."

Dave said, "Come here, Sammy. I'm

sure Mr. Cook didn't mean anything. He was just upset.

"Bill, why don't you take Mr. Cook to the garage? He can change his shirt and pants in there while you wait outside.

"You can put the ruined clothes on the newspapers in the corner."

Mr. Cook went off mumbling, and Bill followed him to the garage.

Five minutes later, Bill came back.

"Any luck?" Dave asked.

"No," said Bill. "Every pocket was empty."

Dave said, "At least we know now that he doesn't carry the letter with him. He will be throwing other clothes on now, and we will have a chance to search my house in a few minutes. You did everything perfectly!"

"Sammy," Bill said. "Thank you for sticking up for me. I hated to shut you up, but I was afraid you'd spill the plans to Mr. Cook."

In a few minutes, Mr. Cook walked up to the children.

He had a fake smile on his face. He had on fresh clothes.

"I'm on my way to the train for a Sunday trip to the city," he said. "I'll be back late tonight, Dave. Be careful with the paint now, boys. No more spills."

He gave a fake laugh and walked away, up the street.

Sammy giggled and said, "He's going for a pretty short ride ... without any money."

Kathy peeked through the bushes.

"He's getting near our side path," she said. "He's slowing down. He ducked into our woods."

They were standing in back of Dave's big house.

It was an old place, three stories high with a basement below. Ted had ordered an elevator built. That way, Dave could get to every floor, even in his wheelchair.

Bill said, "Wow, this place is huge. How many rooms are there?"

"Let's see," Dave answered. "I never counted."

He began to count out loud.

"Seven on the first floor ...

"six on the second floor

"five on the third

"hallways

"... and five in the basement."

"That's twenty-three, all together," Kathy said.

"WOW!" Sammy said. "This is gonna be some big hunt!"

They went inside. Bill said, "If we are going to find the letter this morning, we are going to have to use our heads.

Otherwise we will be searching forever."

Kathy said, "Where does Mr. Cook spend most of his time? Maybe the letter would be there."

Dave said, "He watches TV a lot in his room, or in the breakfast room. He's in the kitchen a lot, or sometimes in the living room or dining room."

"I bet it's in one of those rooms, then," said Bill.

Dave said, "I bet it's up high, where I can't reach."

Sammy said, "Well, I'll start in the kitchen. I like to be near food, in case I get the munchies."

Dave said, "You check out the bathroom, Bill, and the two closets. Kathy can take the dining and breakfast rooms. And I'll look through Mr. Cook's room upstairs."

Kathy said, "What should we say if he

comes back and finds us?"

Dave said, "Just tell him you're waiting for me, Kathy."

"Keep the TV on, so it looks as if you were watching it. Bill will think of something. And of course, Sammy can just say he was hungry."

Sammy began to search.

He searched the refrigerator.

He looked in every pot and pan.

He checked drawers.

He moved onions ...

kitchen tools

... and dish towels.

He stood on the counter to reach the long, open shelf above it.

He searched ...

the bread box

the cans filled with coffee, tea, and beans

... and sugar and flour.

He looked at everything under the sink.

"This is hopeless!" he said to himself. "And besides, I'm STARVING."

He headed for the butler's pantry. It was a small room lined with shelves for food.

Sammy said to himself, "They must have some cookies here. Oh, there's the cookie jar, on that high shelf. I hope it's not empty."

He climbed up and took the cookie jar down.

Kathy heard him and walked in to see what was going on. He handed the jar to her.

"Oh, Sammy," she laughed. "Some detective YOU are!"

"Well, a guy gets hungry sometimes. I don't know why they had to keep the cookies up so high," he complained as he reached inside the jar.

The next minute, he was holding something that wasn't a cookie.

It was a letter. It was addressed to Dave from Ted Stern.

Sammy had found the letter.

Chapter 10:
The Secret Code

Kathy ran to the hall calling, "Dave! Bill! Come quick! Sammy's found it! In a cookie jar!"

Bill ran into the kitchen. He saw Sammy standing there, holding the letter. He gave him a bear hug.

Dave wheeled out of the elevator. "Where in the world was it? Sammy, you're a brain," Dave said.

Bill grinned. "He is the only one smart enough to know to look for a cookie when you're hungry. Quick, Sammy, give it to Dave."

Sammy handed over the letter and then reached into the cookie jar. "Mmm," he said. "Oatmeal."

Dave read the letter out loud as they all crowded around. The letter was short. It said:

Dear Dave,

If I'm in trouble, I hate to see a lad in the sway of trouble, too, so don't forget to take out the garbage from our lunch in the littlest bedroom —Ted

45, 52, 58, 62, 100, 160

"Wow!" said Dave. "This code means he must have had a feeling Mr. Cook couldn't be trusted."

Bill said, "Hey, we'd better copy this quick."

"Why?" said Sammy. "We've got the real letter. Why do we need a copy?"

Bill said, "We can't keep it. Mr. Cook would know we found it."

Dave said, "Here's some paper, Kathy. Can you make an exact copy?"

When Kathy was done, Dave put the real letter back into the cookie jar.

"Here, Sammy," he said. "Be careful when you put this jar back up. If Mr. Cook finds the jar broken, he will know we've seen the letter. We will be in real trouble."

Dave put Kathy's copy into his pants pocket.

Kathy was looking out the window. She said, "Wow! Hurry up! Here he comes now!"

Bill said, "Quick, everyone start eating." He grabbed some bread out of the bread box.

They were all eating when Mr. Cook came in.

He said, "I decided to stay around Bluff Lake today.

"Why are you all inside? Is something wrong?"

Dave said, "No, we were just hungry. Come on everybody. Let's go back out."

They headed for the clubhouse and went inside.

Mr. Cook came out of the house. A white paper was sticking out of his shirt pocket.

Dave said, "There he goes. I bet he's taking the letter to show to Mrs. Tandy."

"Wow!" said Sammy. "Lucky we have the copy!"

Kathy said, "Do you think we can figure it out?"

Dave said, "Let's try right now." He took it out of his pocket. "Hey! Ted showed me this code once!"

Sammy asked, "How does it work? Show us."

Dave said, "First, count the number of letters and spaces and marks, like periods and so on. Add them up. Don't leave out a single space."

They counted and at last agreed there were just 160 things in the letter.

Dave said, "Now use the numbers in pairs. 45 to 52. That's 'a lad in.'

"58 to 62. That's 'sway.'

"100 to 160. That's 'take out the

garbage from our lunch in the littlest bedroom.'"

"Hey," Bill said. "Could the first two parts mean 'Aladin's way'? Aladdin brought things out from an underground cave. But his name is spelled with two *d*'s."

"Maybe. And maybe Ted used only one *d* to make the code hard to break," Dave said.

"And I think the lunch part is a joke Ted used to make."

"Sometimes when we would eat lunch, he would eat everything BUT the bread. He would pick out the cheese and the meat and the lettuce and the tomato.

"Then he would hold up the bread, make a face, and say, 'Do you want this garbage?'"

"Hmm. I think that littlest bedroom must be mine," said Kathy.

Sammy said, "It sounds to me as if we are supposed to be like Aladdin ... in the littlest bedroom ... and take out some bread ... from a cave.

"But you can't do that! There's a basement below, not a cave. And anyway, we are not looking for bread.

"I hate to say it, but that letter just doesn't make any sense."

Bill said, "But it might, Sammy. Bread means money, too. It could even mean jewels."

"Aladdin's way?" said Dave. "I know! In the story, Aladdin found a trap door!"

"A trap door?" said Sammy. "In the littlest bedroom? But I was all over the floor in Kathy's room.

"She let me play with my cars in there. We took the rug up.

"I'd have seen a crack in the floor if there's a trap door."

Kathy said, "Maybe Mrs. Tandy's bedroom is smaller than mine, but I don't think so."

"Maybe Ted's basement office is the littlest bedroom, even though he used it for an office," Sammy said.

Bill said, "Wait a minute. Let Dave think. He knows Ted's house a lot better than we do."

So they all stopped talking.

At last, Dave said, "I've got the answer! The littlest bedroom! It isn't Kathy's, or Mrs. Tandy's, or the basement office. It isn't even a bedroom!"

"Then what is it?" asked Sammy.

"When Ted was adding on his big bedroom to the house, he also added a closet. It's huge, eight by nine feet. It's so big, I used to joke that it wasn't a closet, but a bedroom.

"And under the closet was a dirt

dug-out, with pipes and heating ducts for the new bathroom and bedroom."

"That's it!" Bill said. "There must be a trap door into the dug-out, and when we find it, we will take out bread from a cave."

"Only THIS bread will be diamonds," said Kathy.

"And now the biggest problem of all," said Sammy. "I'm still hungry. When can we go home for lunch?"

Chapter 11:
Aladdin's Way

Bill said, "Let's go home right now. We will phone Mrs. Tandy and tell her we are coming for lunch. That will get Mr. Cook out of the house. But we won't eat.

We will hunt for the trap door."

Sammy said, "YOU might be hunting for the trap door. But I will be eating. Well, I guess I could look and eat at the same time."

Dave said, "I think that will work out fine. Let's go."

As soon as they got home and locked the door, Mrs. Tandy asked, "Any luck, kids? I have our lunch all ready. And my brother is gone."

Dave said, "We found the letter and made a copy, Mrs. Tandy."

She said, "My brother showed me the letter. It didn't make sense."

Dave said, "It was in code. But we've been able to figure it out. The jewels are under the trap door in Ted's big closet."

Mrs. Tandy said, "I KNOW that trap door. I vacuum the carpet over it every week. Come on, I know how to open it."

The closet had a white shag carpet. It had a huge wooden rack with clothes hanging on two sides of it. A tie hanger ran across the third side, between the clothes.

Most of the floor was covered with a clothes hamper and shoe racks.

There was no sign of a trap door.

Bill and Sam and Kathy moved the hamper and the shoe racks out.

Mrs. Tandy pointed. "You just find the edges and lift the whole square of wood and carpet out."

Bill cried out, "I can feel the edge of it!"

Sammy yelled, "All right! I can feel it, too! I bet I could lift it right out myself. It's only about three feet square."

Bill said, "Let's stop right now. We have to plan a little. What if Mr. Cook comes back?"

Sammy said, "I'm getting some food while you plan." He ran to the kitchen.

Mrs. Tandy said, "Who knows when my brother will come back! He's so darned sneaky, he might be hanging around right now."

Dave said, "We will have to split up. Bill and Sammy can go down into the dug-out to look for the jewels. The rest of us should be lookouts."

Mrs. Tandy said, "I'll stay at the back of the house."

Dave said, "I'll be a lookout at the front door."

Kathy said, "How about if I stay outside? That way I can run to the front or back doors if I see him coming."

"Fine," Bill said, "but stay close to the house. If you see any sign of him, run inside. Then we can lock all the doors and phone the police."

Mrs. Tandy said, "That's a good plan. You need to stay safe."

Just then, Sammy came back with the giant dish of sandwiches Mrs. Tandy had made, and two flashlights.

He said, "No sense starving to death while we search."

Dave said, "Let's go to our lookout spots." He, Kathy, and Mrs. Tandy left the room.

Bill said, "Well, let's get started."

They pulled on the trap door.

The section of floor lifted slightly.

"This is HEAVY," puffed Sammy.

At last, they slid the section out of place. Below was a deep black hole.

They shined their flashlights in.

Inside the dug-out were pipes ...

a big metal hot-air duct

... and wires running near the walls and ceiling.

The ground was covered with sharp gray stones and junk left over from when the closet was built.

Sammy asked, "How will we get down?"

Bill said, "It looks about five feet deep. I think we can just slide in feet first.

"Here I go."

He slid down. Sammy handed him a flashlight.

"All set," Bill said. "I'll help you down."

Sammy slid in.

They shined their lights around.

The dug-out was bigger than they had expected it to be. It ran under the bathroom, too. But they had to bend over to walk in it.

The walls were made of concrete.

Sammy said, "Hey, this is like a jail with no windows. And it smells like a mushroom. Let's do this fast. I hate it in here."

Bill said, "Look in that pile of old rags first. Then let's lift all the little pieces of board."

"OK," Sammy agreed.

There was nothing on the ground.

They looked around the pipes where they went into the wall. Nothing.

The ceiling was like a porch ceiling, with boards nailed across it to hold up the floor above.

The boys shined their lights up, between the boards. A bag of jewels might be hanging there. Nothing.

Every time they crossed under the hot-air duct, they had to bend way down.

Then Bill said, "Wait a minute. We've looked everywhere except on TOP of the hot-air duct."

Sammy said, "I'm not going to put MY hands up there! If I were a spider, that's where I'd be waiting for a nice, yummy hand."

Bill said, "Let's take some little boards and poke around."

They did, and in a minute, Bill poked something that slid with a thundering

noise across the duct. They saw it stick out on the other side.

It was a large wooden box!

Suddenly, Sammy climbed out of the dug-out and ran to the phone.

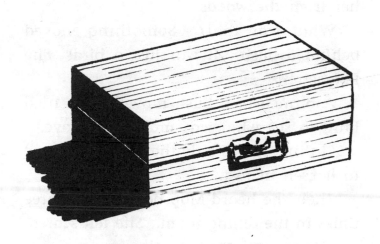

Chapter 12:
The Jewels at Last

At the very same time the boys found the box, Mrs. Tandy was standing inside the back door looking out the window.

She hoped her brother could not see her from the woods.

What was that? Something moved behind a bush. It was just a bird! She felt better!

A branch of a bush moved. She tried hard to see what was making it move.

"I think it was only the wind," she said to herself at last.

Then she heard Mop bark two or three times in the dining room. She felt scared.

"He must hear something move outside that we don't."

She took a look into the dining room. Dave was sitting at the open front door.

He didn't see anything wrong. He didn't hear anything wrong. But Mop barked again.

Suddenly, a person's head showed at a window near Dave's door.

Dave spun his chair back, to slam the

door. Then he stopped. The face at the window was Kathy's.

She ran in the front door. All she said was, "I think he's got a gun!"

Mrs. Tandy ran into the dining room. She pulled Kathy away from the door and shouted, "Get down! This has gone far enough! We need to call Chief ..."

Suddenly, a man jumped out of the bushes and up onto the front porch.

Dave shouted, "Get away from here, Mr. Cook!"

Mr. Cook stepped closer.

He said, "Just a minute there. You can't send me away. Ted Stern hired me."

Dave said, "Well, I'M firing you."

He slammed the door. Mr. Cook pushed it open before Dave was able to lock it.

Mr. Cook said, "You can't stop me, you stupid kid! I'm coming in."

Behind him, Dave saw another man
running up the driveway from the woods.

Dave rolled his chair hard at Mr. Cook.
The footrest hit him right in the shins.

Mr. Cook yelped, "Ouch!" and bent
down.

Now the other man ran up onto the
porch. It was Chief Hemster.

"Well, Dave," said the police chief.
"Someone named Sammy just phoned in

a nine-one-one. He said there might be some trouble here at the house."

The chief looked at Mr. Cook. "What happened here? It looked as if you were trying to break in."

Mr. Cook looked at Chief Hemster and blinked.

"This woman ... this Mrs. Tandy is turning these kids against me," he said. "After all I've done for Dave. Did you see him ram his wheelchair into me?"

Dave said, "Chief, he has a gun. And his name isn't really Al Cook."

Mrs. Tandy said, "It's Fred Wilson. He's my long-lost brother."

Mr. Cook said, "Becky! You're turning against your own brother?"

Chief Hemster patted Mr. Cook's pants pockets and found a small dark gun.

"You are under arrest, Al Cook ... or whatever your name is."

He handcuffed Mr. Cook.

Chief Hemster spoke into his radio.

"Officer? Bring the car into the driveway. We need to take someone to the station for questioning."

He left with Mr. Cook in the police car.

Dave asked, "Where are Sammy and Bill?"

But just then, Bill and Sammy came running in.

They were dirty. They had cobwebs in their hair.

Bill had popped a button off and was holding up his pants.

Sammy's hair stuck out like a bunch of weeds.

One of his shoes had fallen off when he scrambled out of the dug-out. He stood there with one foot bare.

They both had grins on their faces ... from ear to ear.

Bill and Sammy held a box made of wood. It was about as big as two shoeboxes tied together.

"We found it! We found it!" Sammy shouted. "We found the jewels! And I kept Bill from being killed by the spiders!"

He put down the box and opened the top. "Look!"

Inside were small brown envelopes.

Sammy opened one. It had a big, sparkling green stone in it, carved to look like a man's head.

"That's it!" said Dave. He looked into another envelope. "Look! This one has diamonds in it."

Everyone began looking into the envelopes.

Then Bill said, "Wait. Should we open them all? What do we do next, Dave?"

Sammy butted in. "What do we do next? I know what to do next!"

He ran into the big bedroom.

He ran back in a minute. He had the plate with the sandwiches.

"We have LUNCH next, that's what we do," he said. "We never DID eat these and I'm STARVING."

So when Chief Hemster got back from the station, he found the Woodlanders sitting around the kitchen table.

They were having a party.

There were the sandwiches. And an ice cream cake from the freezer. And a bowl of popcorn.

The big wooden box sat in the middle of the table. On a plate on top of it was a big glass pitcher of lemonade.

"Now," the chief said, "it's time you told me what's been going on around here.

"I've had a heck of a time getting a straight story from Al Cook ... or Fred

Wilson ... or whatever his name is. Do you know he didn't even have a wallet with ID cards?"

Everyone at the table began to giggle. Then they began to laugh really hard.

Sammy was laughing so hard, he fell off his chair. He landed with one foot in Mop's water bowl.

Mrs. Tandy stood up to help him out. She tipped over the popcorn.

Popcorn rained all over the floor. Mop began to eat it up.

Bill jumped up to stop Mop, and one of his hands went right into the ice cream cake.

Ice cream splashed onto Kathy's hair.

At last, Chief Hemster gave up on them. He cut himself a slice of cake. He pulled his chair away from the table.

"This is better than watching cartoons on TV," he said.

And he sat back eating, and watching the Woodlanders' funny, messy, happy party.

Chapter 13:
Together at Last

At last the party was over.

Mop lay on his back. His popcorn belly stuck up in the air. He was asleep and snoring doggy snores.

The children told Chief Hemster what had been going on.

Then Bill opened the box again.

Kathy asked, "What is that paper sticking up from below the jewels?"

Bill said, "It's for Dave."

Dave opened it. Inside it said:

Dear Dave,

You will be reading this letter only if something has happened to me. I love you as if you were my son. So I am giving you one-fourth of these jewels. That way, you will have plenty of money to go to college and to take care of yourself for life.

I am giving the same amount, one-fourth of the jewels, to each of my sister's children, Bill, Sammy, and Kathy.

I ask that Mrs. Tandy be your helper as you grow up. I have put money into the bank for her.

Stay happy and good and busy.

Love,

Ted

By the time Dave finished reading the letter, Mrs. Tandy was crying.

Chief Hemster and Kathy were both patting her back.

The chief said, "I'm so sorry, Becky. I know how much you cared for Mr. Stern. He was a fine man.

"And this letter shows how much he loved you all. Let's get the jewels taken care of. He'd want us to."

They made a list of the jewels.

Then they rode to the bank, and put the jewels into a bank box.

Then they went to Dave's house and got all the things he wanted to move to Uncle Ted's house.

They called the newspaper. They put in an ad to rent Dave's house to a new family.

An hour later, a big truck stopped near Uncle Ted's backyard.

Five moving men stepped out. They carried out Dave's heavy gym equipment.

They took it down the ramp to the basement.

Then Dave said, "This next thing is a surprise from me, to us."

The men slid a metal ramp out of the back of the truck.

The children could hear a bumping sound. They could hear the men grunting with effort. Whatever they were moving, it was BIG.

Suddenly, they came through the woods rolling a platform on big iron wheels.

On it was ... the clubhouse!

Bill shouted. He began dancing around the grass. He forgot he was fourteen and very grown up. He did six somer-saults and a cart-wheel.

The men placed the clubhouse in the yard near the woods.

Sammy was so happy, of course, he had to hop around and dance, too.

He bumped up against Bill and knocked him down.

Bill said, "Thanks a lot, Sammy."

Sammy said, "I did it because I like you." He helped Bill up.

Bill said, "Kathy and I will make you a smooth path to the clubhouse door, Dave."

Sammy said, "And I'll plant flowers around it."

"And I'm going to go into it and eat all these cookies myself," said a voice from the house.

Mrs. Tandy marched out of the back door with a giant-size plate of cookies, and walked straight into the clubhouse.

The children rushed after her. They lifted Dave in his chair into the clubhouse.

Soon, around the clubhouse table, talking and laughing and eating cookies, sat the happy Woodlanders.

They all knew it was the start of something wonderful.